George Brown, CLASS CLOWN

The Twelve Burps of Christmas

For Liz Barkan, whose warmth and workouts
melt away the winter aches—NK

For Mom and Dad, for making
every Christmas magical and for
never giving me a Red Ryder BB Gun—AB

GROSSET & DUNLAP
Published by the Penguin Group
Penguin Group (USA) Inc., 375 Hudson Street, New York,
New York 10014, USA
Penguin Group (Canada), 90 Eglinton Avenue East, Suite 700,
Toronto, Ontario M4P 2Y3, Canada
(a division of Pearson Penguin Canada Inc.)
Penguin Books Ltd., 80 Strand, London WC2R 0RL, England
Penguin Group Ireland, 25 St. Stephen's Green, Dublin 2, Ireland
(a division of Penguin Books Ltd.)
Penguin Group (Australia), 250 Camberwell Road, Camberwell,
Victoria 3124, Australia
(a division of Pearson Australia Group Pty. Ltd.)
Penguin Books India Pvt. Ltd., 11 Community Centre, Panchsheel Park,
New Delhi—110 017, India
Penguin Group (NZ), 67 Apollo Drive, Rosedale,
Auckland 0632, New Zealand
(a division of Pearson New Zealand Ltd.)
Penguin Books (South Africa) (Pty.) Ltd., 24 Sturdee Avenue,
Rosebank, Johannesburg 2196, South Africa

Penguin Books Ltd., Registered Offices:
80 Strand, London WC2R 0RL, England

Text copyright © 2012 by Nancy Krulik. Illustrations copyright © 2012
by Aaron Blecha. All rights reserved. Published by Grosset & Dunlap,
a division of Penguin Young Readers Group, 345 Hudson Street,
New York, New York 10014. GROSSET & DUNLAP is a trademark of
Penguin Group (USA) Inc. Printed in the U.S.A.

Library of Congress Control Number: 2011046446

ISBN 978-0-448-45680-5   10 9 8 7 6 5 4 3 2

ALWAYS LEARNING   **PEARSON**

George Brown, CLASS CLOWN
The Twelve Burps of Christmas

by Nancy Krulik
illustrated by Aaron Blecha

Grosset & Dunlap
An Imprint of Penguin Group (USA) Inc.

Don't Be Such a Flake

Chapter 1

"Yuck!"

George Brown looked down at the plate of red and green Jell-O with pieces of fruit in it. The Jell-O was the lunch lady's way of getting everyone into the **Christmas spirit**. Not that the kids at Edith B. Sugarman Elementary School needed reminding. Christmas was all anyone could talk about these days.

"I'm getting a battery-operated guitar amp and a wireless microphone," Louie told a bunch of other fourth-graders. "And a new air hockey table for the game room."

"How do you know you're definitely getting all that?" Julianna asked him.

"Because they're on my Christmas list," Louie said.

"Don't you know anything?" Louie's friend Mike asked Julianna.

"Louie *always* gets what's on the list," his pal Max added.

"Well, **exc-u-u-u-se me**," Julianna said.

George turned to Julianna. "I spent the whole weekend trying to find gifts my mother has hidden. **But no luck.**"

"Oh, *Georgie* . . . look over here."

Oh man. It was Sage walking toward their table. She was dangling some green leafy thing in the air.

"Do you know what this is?" Sage asked. She batted her eyelashes. "And do you know what it *means*?"

George knew what it was. **It was mistletoe.** He also knew what it meant.

Sage wanted him to kiss her. That was not going to happen, **not in this life**.

Sage puckered up her mouth.

George took a big bite of his macaroni and cheese and shoved a spoonful of Jell-O into his mouth. "Sure. I know what it is," George answered. **Jell-O goo, slimy yellow cheese, and chewed-up fruit bits dripped out of his mouth and onto his chin.**

"Yuck!" Sage shouted. She dropped the mistletoe and walked away. "Never mind."

Score one for George. He swallowed his food and grinned.

"Sage's a real pain," George's best friend, Alex, said.

"She's not the biggest problem," George told him.

Alex knew what George meant. "You're worried about the you-know-whats," he whispered.

George nodded. Alex was his only friend who knew about the **you-know-whats**. That was because it was a tale too terrible to tell. But Alex had been smart enough to figure it out on his own. The you-know-whats were magic burps, **burps so huge and powerful that they were ruining George's life**.

It all started when George and his family first moved to Beaver Brook. George's dad was in the army, so the family moved around a lot. By now, George understood that first days at school could be pretty rotten. But *this* first day was the rottenest.

In his old school, George had been the class clown. He was always pulling pranks and making jokes. But George had promised himself that things were going to be different at Edith B. Sugarman Elementary School. He was turning over a new leaf. **No more pranks.** No more whoopee cushions or spitballs shot through straws. No more bunny ears behind people's heads in class pictures. No more goofing on teachers when their backs were turned.

But George didn't have to be a math whiz like Alex to figure out how many friends you make being the unfunny, well-behaved new kid in school. The answer was easy. **Zero. Nada. Zilch.**

That night, George's parents took him out to Ernie's Ice Cream Emporium. While they were sitting outside and George was finishing his root

beer float, a shooting star **flashed across the sky**. So George made a wish.

I want to make kids laugh—but not get into trouble.

Unfortunately, the star was gone before George could finish the wish. So only half came true—**the first half**.

A minute later, George had a funny feeling in his belly. It was like there were hundreds of tiny bubbles bouncing around in there. The bubbles hopped up and down and all around. They ping-ponged their way into his chest and bing-bonged their way up into his throat. And then . . .

 **B-U-U-U-R-P!**

George let out a big burp. A *huge* burp. **A SUPER burp!**

The super burp was loud, and it was *magic*.

Suddenly, George lost control of his arms and legs. It was like they had minds of their own. His hands grabbed straws and stuck them up his nose like a walrus. His feet jumped up on the table and started dancing the hokey pokey. Everyone at Ernie's Ice Cream Emporium started laughing—**except George's parents**.

The magical super burps came back lots of times after that. And every time a burp arrived, it brought trouble with it. Like the time George **dive-bombed into the audience** in the middle of the school talent show. That wouldn't have been so bad if he hadn't landed right in Principal McKeon's arms!

George would never forget the time a burp exploded during Louie's birthday party at a water park. George went crazy on a tubing ride. **He dived underwater and started pinching people's butts!** Boy, were the lifeguards mad.

There were a lot of good surprises that could come during Christmas. Surprise presents. Surprise visitors. Surprise snowstorms. Those were great.

But **a surprise burp** was definitely *not* something he wanted!

"Have you burped a lot lately?" Alex whispered to George.

"Not since last Sunday, when it made me **soak my feet in my soup bowl** during dinner," George said.

"I'm working on a cure," Alex assured him. "Maybe that can be my Christmas present to you."

George smiled. **A cure for the super burp.** That would be the best Christmas present *ever*!

Chapter 2

"Class, settle down," Mrs. Kelly, George's teacher, said as the kids filed into the classroom after music class.

George hated music class. Today Mrs. Cadenza had taught them "The Snowflake Serenade." The words were: *Snow is falling everywhere, snowflakes flying in the air. Landing softly on a branch, dancing a lovely snowflake dance.*

Sheesh. **It didn't even rhyme.** So George had made up his own words in his head while everyone else sang out

loud: *Snowflakes falling everywhere, in my ears and on my hair. Melting as they end their dance. Looks like Louie wet his pants!*

Now *that* would have been fun to sing!

"I have a wonderful holiday surprise," Mrs. Kelly said. "I call it our Santa's Workshop project because it's all about toys!" She gave the kids a gummy smile. "Over the next two nights, your homework will be to research the history of your favorite toy. On Friday, you will have the chance to tell the class what you've learned."

George slumped down in his seat. A research project? That was her big holiday surprise? Mrs. Kelly sure had a weird way of saying "Merry Christmas."

At least George had no trouble deciding what he'd write about— skateboards. **He loved to skateboard.** And he already had a great idea: He would demonstrate riding a skateboard *during* his speech. **That meant that practicing on his skateboard would actually be doing homework!**

That was why, for the first time in a long time, George wanted to start working on his homework right after school. But his mom had other plans for him. She wanted to take George shopping at Mabel's Department Store.

The last time he was at Mabel's, the burp had made him run up the down escalator, crashing into people and sending their packages flying.

George wouldn't be surprised if Mabel's Department Store had **wanted posters** with his picture all over the store.

"I don't want to go shopping," George groaned as his mother pulled the car into the parking lot.

"But I have to get gifts for Grandma and Great-Aunt Catherine," his mom explained.

"Why do you need me?" George asked.

"Well . . ." His mother gave him **a weird smile**.

Uh-oh. George had seen that smile before. His mother used it every time she wanted George to do something he was sure to hate.

"For a picture on Santa's lap," his mother said.

George's eyes nearly bugged out of his head. Was she kidding? That was for little kids! George wasn't going to climb up on Santa's lap. "No way. *Not happening.*"

"Oh, come on. I've kept every picture of you with Santa since you were a baby." His mother sighed. "Soon you're going to be too big."

Soon? George was *already* too big!

But George's mom really wanted him to pose for that picture. And George didn't want to disappoint her, especially not this close to Christmas. **That would be a bad move.**

"Okay, I guess," George said.

They walked into the store. Right away, George spotted a saleswoman who had been there the day of his big burp. Quickly, George wrapped his scarf over his mouth and nose and pulled his ski cap down to his eyebrows. The only things showing were his eyes. There was no way she could recognize him now.

"What are you doing?" George's mom asked.

"I'm cold," George said from under his scarf.

"You're not wearing all that when you take your picture," his mom said. "I want to be able to see **your beautiful smile**."

She wanted him to smile, too? Now *that* was asking a lot.

There was a long line of little kids waiting to see **Santa at the North Pole Photo Studio**. The studio was on the eighth floor of Mabel's Department Store, right next to the toy department. That

meant the kids were all staring at all those toys while they waited in line—when they weren't staring at Santa, that is. Once George had believed that the guy sitting in the big chair was the real Santa. **Now he knew better.** Still, George didn't want to ruin it for all the little kids. So he kept his mouth shut.

"Ho, ho, ho," the department store Santa said when it was finally George's turn. "You're a big one."

"My mom wants a picture," George said, plopping onto his lap.

"Ho, ho, ho." The store Santa laughed again. "What do you want for Christmas?"

No department store Santa was going to be able to get him what he really wanted.

Especially right at that very moment, since suddenly **the super burp was back** and on the move! Already, tiny bubbles were bouncing around inside George. They were kickboxing his kidneys, ping-ponging past his pancreas, and loop-the-looping around his liver.

George shut his mouth tight to keep the burp from escaping. **But the burp was strong.** It jingle-jangled its way into his throat. And then . . .

George let out a burp so loud, elves at the North Pole could have heard it!

"Whoa!" The department store Santa pinched his nose. "What'd you have for lunch, sonny? That was some strong burp!"

George opened his mouth to say "Excuse me." But that's not what came out. Instead, his mouth shouted, "Ho, ho, ho!"

George's hands took on a life of their own. They reached up and **grabbed Santa's red cap** and plopped it onto George's head. George's legs leaped from Santa's lap. His feet started running all around the North Pole Photo Studio.

"George!" his mother shouted. "Sit back down on Santa's lap **this instant**!"

"Ho, ho, ho!" George's mouth

shouted to all the little kids in line.
"Merry Christmas!"

"Give me back that hat!" the
department store Santa shouted.
"Stop that brat!"

A little boy waiting in line said,
"Mama, Santa called that boy a brat."

"Santa is being mean," a little girl said.

George's feet ran around the
North Pole Photo Studio, knocking
over cardboard candy canes. His hands
grabbed ornaments off a plastic tree and
tossed silver tinsel in the air.

"Ho, ho, ho!" George's mouth
laughed. "'Tis the season to be jolly!"

"Somebody get him!" Santa shouted.

One of Santa's helpers tried to grab George.

"Ho, ho, ho!" George's mouth shouted as his feet started to run.

Whoops! George's feet tripped on some slippery tinsel.

Bash! George fell to the ground.

Crash! **The Christmas tree fell over.** Christmas decorations and tinsel went flying all over the place.

Whoosh! Suddenly George felt the air rush right out of him. It was like someone had popped a balloon in his belly. The super burp was gone! But George was still there, covered in tinsel and holding two red Christmas balls.

A little girl with long, brown curls looked at him strangely. "Are you one of Santa's helpers?" she asked.

"No, he's not," the department store Santa said. He turned to George's mother. "Get this kid out of here," he added.

The photographer handed her a picture of George on Santa's lap. George peered over his mother's shoulder. There he was, with his mouth wide open and his eyes bulging out of his head. Santa was holding his nose. George had a feeling that was not the Christmas picture his mom had in mind.

George's mom looked at the picture.
Then she looked at George all covered
in tinsel. "Gee, George," she said. "If
you didn't want to pose with Santa, you
should have just said so."

Chapter 3

"Another burp in Mabel's?" Alex whispered to George as the boys filed into the school auditorium the next morning.

George nodded. **"It was a whopper."**

"I did more research last night," Alex said. "Did you know that certain species of birds use burping as mating calls?"

"Interesting. But what about **a cure**?" George asked.

Alex shook his head. "Nothing yet."

Just then, Alex and George's friend Chris joined them. Chris was in another fourth-grade class, so the boys usually only saw him at lunch. "Do you guys have any idea why we're here?" Chris asked Alex and George.

George shook his head. "Mrs. Kelly just said we should go straight to the auditorium."

"It's about **the holiday play**," Louie said, pushing past the boys and interrupting their conversation. "When my big brother, Sam, was in fourth grade, they did a holiday play. Sam was the narrator. He had more lines than anyone. Sam's a great actor."

"I hate plays." Alex groaned. "I'm no good at acting or singing."

"I always forget my lines," Chris said. He looked at Alex. "You remember the play about the parts of speech last year? All I had to say was, 'A noun is a person, place, or thing.'"

"And you said, 'A noun is a *place mat or something*,'" Louie said and started **laughing hysterically**.

Chris turned red. "I was nervous."

"And he wasn't wrong," Alex added. "A place mat is a thing, and that makes it a noun."

George hated plays, too. It wasn't that he didn't like singing or that he couldn't learn lines. **Plays took place onstage, and the super burp seemed to really like stages.** It had already burst out at the talent show and right before the county-wide spelling bee. It seemed the bigger the audience, the bigger the burp—and the more embarrassed George wound up.

"Oh, *Georgie*," Sage called suddenly from the back of the auditorium. "Wait up. **Save a seat for me.**"

"Like *that's* happening," George said. He hurried into the row where Julianna was sitting and took the seat next to her. Alex and Chris sat down next to George. Sage was three people away.

Mrs. Kelly stepped onto the stage. She walked over to the microphone and tapped on it twice. Then she used her sleeve to wipe some smudges off her glasses and looked at her clipboard.

"As some of you may know, it is a tradition here at Edith B. Sugarman for the fourth grade to put on **a Holiday Spectacular** for the whole school."

Louie turned around from the row in front of George and his friends. "See? What'd I tell you?"

"Mrs. Cadenza will be the music director, and I will be your choreographer and director."

"Choreographer? **That means she's going to make us dance in front of everyone**," Julianna said with a frown.

"This is going to be a *nightmare*," Alex agreed. "I can't dance."

"Everyone has a part. So don't worry.

Nobody will be left out," Mrs. Kelly said. "Mrs. Cadenza is passing around the cast list now."

A minute later, George stared at the paper that his music teacher had handed him. He looked for his name. "Oh man," he complained. "This stinks. **I'm a snowflake.**"

"Georgie, I'm a snowflake, too!" Sage **squealed** loudly. Quickly, she traded seats with Julianna, so she could be closer to George. "We're going to have so much fun rehearsing together. Maybe we can practice after school, too."

George sank down in his chair and buried his face in his hands.

"Look. There are six snowflakes," Alex told him, pointing at the cast list. "You won't even have to talk to Sage. **It won't be so bad.**"

"Easy for you to say," George said. "You're one of, like, twenty carolers. Carolers don't dance. You can stand in the back and move your lips without really singing."

"I don't think I'm dancing, either," Chris said. "It says I'm a hibernating bear. **I don't think you can dance when you're hibernating.**"

"Lucky you," Julianna said. "I'm stuck singing that dumb 'Happy Elves' song we learned in music class. I'm singing it as a trio with Max and Mike."

"Max and Mike are singing without Louie? I didn't think they could *breathe* without him," George commented.

Louie turned around again and smiled. "I'm singing 'Cold Winter Wind.' *I've* got a solo."

"He *should* sing solo," George whispered to Alex, Chris, and Julianna. **"So *low* we can't hear him."**

George's friends all laughed.

"It's kind of strange, isn't it," George went on, "that Mrs. Kelly has Louie singing a song about cold air when he's usually so full of hot air."

"What's so funny?" Louie demanded.

George was on a roll. Louie was so easy to goof on. But George didn't make any more jokes about him. He was trying to be the new, improved George. And that meant not making fun of anyone. **Not even Louie.** At least not out loud, anyway.

"We do a **Winter Wonderland Watusi** while we sing that snow song," George groaned to Chris and Alex as they walked home from school later that afternoon. "I hate that snow song."

"You guys want to come over for a while?" Alex asked.

"Sure. For a little bit," Chris answered.

"I'm going home," George said. "My mom's at work. **This is the perfect time for present hunting!**" And there was no ice on the streets, so maybe he'd have time for some skateboarding, too.

When George got home, **he didn't even stop to have a snack**. He just started looking around the house in all the places that might be hiding a Christmas present. He searched under all the beds, in every drawer, and in the closets. He even looked in the clothes dryer. But there were no gift boxes.

George was just about to give up when **he spotted something red and green** hidden under a pile of dirty laundry next to the washer. Sure enough, there it was: a green and red box with a card that read FOR GEORGE.

Oh yeah! The box was just the right size and shape for **a black leather skateboarding jacket**. Or for that way-cool gray hoodie with the skeleton on it. For months he'd been hinting that he wanted it. Quickly, George lifted the lid off the box and peeked inside.

There was no jacket. No hoodie. Instead, there was a green and red sweater with Rudolph the Red-Nosed Reindeer knit into the front. Rudolph's nose was a red pom-pom. **It was the ugliest thing George had ever seen.**

Chapter 4

"Hi, Mom," George said as he walked into his mom's craft store, the Knit Wit, after dinner that night. "Something came up and Dad had to go to the army base, so he dropped me off and—**ta da!**—here I am."

"Hi, honey," George's mom answered without looking up. She was wrapping a gift. She couldn't stop for even a minute. There was a whole line of people waiting. "You can go do your homework in the back."

"Already did it," George told her. And he had. George knew all there was to know about skateboards now. **He'd even practiced two new moves to show the class.**

George looked at the long line. "You need help?"

"Um, no thanks, honey," she said.

George figured his mom was probably remembering the last time he'd helped out. A super burp had hit, and it was just lucky his mom was still in business.

"I'll do a good job," George promised. **"I won't cause trouble."**

George's mom sighed. "Okay. I really do need the help," she said finally. "Why don't you take over wrapping gifts while I work the cash register?"

"You've got it," George said happily. He loved wrapping gifts. It was like doing an art project. He stepped behind the counter and took a box of beads from the next customer. Then he began folding and taping the wrapping paper around the gift. He finished it all off by sticking **a red bow right on top**. "Next!" George cried out happily.

George had wrapped three or four presents when **suddenly something terrible happened**. The store door opened. And then . . .

"Hi, *Georgie!*"

It was Sage. There was **no escaping** her. Not even here, in the safety of his mother's store.

George stayed focused on the knit-a-poncho kit he was wrapping. *Fold over the edges. Tape the sides. Add the bow.*

"Oh, I see you're busy, *Georgie*," Sage said. "I'll shop for a while with my mom, and then I'll come talk to you."

Don't do me any favors, George thought to himself. But out loud he just said, "Next!"

A woman placed a make-your-own-stained-glass kit on the counter. George unrolled a big piece of green wrapping paper and placed it under the box. He reached for the tape. And then something started to happen. Something **even worse than seeing Sage** come through that door.

There were bubbles bouncing around in his belly. Bing-bong. Ping-pong. The bubbles were big. They were strong. And they could only mean one thing: **The super burp was back!**

George couldn't let that burp slip from his lips. Not after he'd promised his mom there would be no trouble. Quickly, he grabbed the tape dispenser and pulled off a long piece. He placed the tape right over his lips and sealed them shut. But those bubbles kept bouncing around and pushing on his lips, searching for one little opening.

And there it was. Right on the side of his mouth. Bing-bong. Ping-pong. The bubbles were looking for **an escape hatch**!

George reached for another piece of tape. Oh no! The dispenser was empty. George *had* to seal his lips shut. But how?

And Sage was heading in his direction again. **Double trouble!**

Suddenly, George's eyes fell on the pile of bows with sticky backings. Quickly, he grabbed **a big red one**, peeled off the backing, and smacked it on his lips. The bubbles bounced hard against the bow. And then . . .

Whoosh! George felt the air rush right out of him. It was as if someone had popped a balloon right in the middle of his belly. The super burp was gone!

Unfortunately, Sage was still there. "That's just what I want for Christmas," she squealed. "*Georgie,* all wrapped up with a big red bow."

Oh man. **How embarrassing.**

"Isn't that sweet?" one woman said.

"They're such cute kids," another added.

Ordinarily, that would have made George really, really mad. But not now. George had *squelched the belch.* **And that was all that mattered.**

On Friday morning, Sage told everyone about how *Georgie* had wrapped himself up as a gift, **just for her.**

"Dude, for real?" Alex asked as the boys took their seats in Mrs. Kelly's classroom.

"Of course not. I was trying to stop the burp," George explained. "I sealed up my mouth with a bow."

"Oh," Alex nodded. "That makes more sense. "

"And I beat it," George said proudly. "But it wasn't easy. You've got to find a cure, fast! **Sage thinks I *like* her.** That's one of the meanest tricks the burp has ever played on me."

"Okay, class," Mrs. Kelly said. "Take your seats. I can't wait to hear your oral reports. Who would like to go first?"

George shot his hand up in the air. So did Louie, Sage, and Julianna.

"Julianna, why don't you start us off?" Mrs. Kelly said.

George frowned. But he didn't say anything. He would wait his turn—like a new, improved, well-behaved George.

Julianna held up her wooden

boomerang.
"Boomerangs are very popular in Australia. But ancient ones have been found in parts of Europe and Asia," she explained. "King Tut had a collection of them when he ruled Egypt. And even though we think of them as toys, boomerangs can be used for hunting."

George had to admit, **the boomerang was cool**. But his skateboard was even cooler. Wait until the kids saw him **pop a wheelie** right in the classroom!

Mrs. Kelly chose Sage to go after Julianna.

"Dolls are the oldest toys in the history of the world. Girls have been

playing with them since prehistoric times,"
Sage told the class. "In ancient Greece,
girls would make clothes for their dolls
and dress them up. Dolls are important for
learning as well as playing because they
teach girls how to be moms."

George pulled out a pen and started
drawing **a skeleton tattoo** on his arm.
Sage's report was the most boring ever!

When Sage *finally* finished her report
about dolls, Mrs. Kelly asked Louie to talk
about *his* favorite toy. Louie walked up to
the front of the room and
pulled a **red and yellow
yo-yo** from his
pocket. "The
yo-yo is the
second-oldest
toy in history,
right after
the doll,"

Louie said. "Kids in ancient Greece played with yo-yos made from clay and wood and . . ."

George was trying to pay attention to Louie. **He really was.** But it was hard because of what was going on inside his belly. There were bubbles yo-yoing up and down in there. And that could mean only one thing: The magical super burp was back. *Again.* **Didn't it ever take a break?**

Boing-bong. Ping-pong. The burp was already kicking at George's kidneys and rocketing against his ribs. Quickly, George rolled up a wad of paper and shoved it inside his mouth like a cork.

But the burp wasn't going to give up so fast. It bounced on George's tongue **like a trampoline**. And then . . .

The paper cork **burst out of George's mouth**—and hit Sage right in the back of the head.

"Ow!" Sage turned and looked at George. "Why did you do that, *Georgie*?"

"Oh no, dude," Alex whispered to him.

Oh *yes*, dude.

Louie tried to ignore the sound of the burp. "There are hundreds of yo-yo tricks," he said, continuing his report. "The first trick I learned was how to make it sleep."

That was all the super burp had to hear. **George's nose went nuts and started snoring.** *"Zzzzzz. Zzzzzz."*

The kids laughed. Well, all except Louie. He yelled, "George, stop acting all weird!"

"George, please," Mrs. Kelly said. "Don't interrupt. Go on, Louie."

"And this trick is called **skin the cat**," Louie continued. "You start by making your yo-yo sleep—"

Before Louie could go any further, George sprang up onto Mrs. Kelly's desk. *"Meow. Meow!* He skinned me!" **George hissed like an angry cat.** *"Meow!"*

The kids were really cracking up now.

Whoosh! All the air rushed out of George. It was as if someone had popped a balloon in his belly.

The super burp was gone. But George was **still sitting on Mrs. Kelly's desk**!

"George, get down," Mrs. Kelly said.

George did as he was told.

"I don't know why you do these silly things," Mrs. Kelly told him. "But I can't have you ruining everyone's presentations. Please go down to Principal McKeon's office."

"But I have my skateboard . . ."

48

George began. But he could tell by the look on Mrs. Kelly's face that he wasn't going to be **popping any wheelies** today. The only popping he'd be doing was popping down to the principal's office. *Again.*

Chapter 5

"Is everybody ready to **deck the halls**?" Mr. Buttonwood, the leader of Beaver Scout Troop 307, asked that evening. The troop was going to decorate yards around town. The people who wanted their yards decorated were leaving notes in their mailboxes asking the Beaver Scouts to hang **Christmas ornaments and tinsel** on their trees.

"This was a great idea, Julianna," George said as he gathered up a bag of ornaments.

"It seemed like a fun way to earn our Good Neighbor scout badges," Julianna said. "I made some God's-eye ornaments from string and Popsicle sticks to hang on trees. My parents learned how to do it when they were visiting the Huichol tribe in Mexico."

"I brought popcorn strands," Chris said. "They're a gift for **hungry birds**. Nobody ever thinks of them at Christmas."

"That's true," Alex agreed. "I'll help you string them on the branches."

"Did you see the ornament *I* made, Georgie?" Sage asked him. She held up a red plastic heart.

"Hearts are for Valentine's Day," George said.

"I know," Sage said. "I can't wait for **our first Valentine's Day together**."

George ignored Sage and said, "Oh look, more stuff."

Max and Mike were lugging huge bags of ornaments.

"Be careful not to break anything," Louie told them.

"We're hanging all these ornaments for Louie," Max and Mike said together.

"Then what are *you* doing to earn your **Good Neighbor badge**?" Alex asked Louie.

"I'll tell them where to hang everything," Louie explained. "I have a good eye for that. For instance, I know the angel needs to go on the top of the tree. Also, I have to be careful with my hands," Louie explained. "What if I hurt one of my fingers hanging a Christmas ball? How will I play the guitar when I sing my solo in the Holiday Spectacular?" Then he turned to George. **"I bet you're already practicing how you're going to mess it up."**

George couldn't think of anything to say back. There had been a rehearsal at the end of the school day, and it had gone fine. As bad as being a snowflake was, George would be happy to sing and do the Watusi if only he didn't wind up **going wacko in front of the whole school**.

"Okay, gang. Ready to leave?" Troop Leader Buttonwood called out, and then he slid on an open roll of ribbon.

"Whoa!" *Thud.* "OUCH!"

The kids all came running to help Troop Leader Buttonwood to his feet.

"Are you all right?" Sage asked him. The troop leader **rubbed his rear end**.

"I'm fine," he said. "I meant to trip on that.

I was showing you kids that it's dangerous to leave stuff on the ground."

A few minutes later, George and the other Beaver Scouts were all busy hanging ornaments and stringing ropes of tinsel on trees in families' yards. It felt good to be doing something nice for his neighbors. Especially since the neighbors had been rewarding the scouts with yummy treats! **Already George had eaten two candy canes, a huge chocolate chip cookie, a peppermint patty, and a piece of fruitcake.**

"This is awesome," George said as he popped the last bit of cake into his mouth. "We should do it every year."

"There's my house!" Louie shouted suddenly, pointing down the road. "See it? The mansion with all the Christmas lights?

My dad goes really crazy at Christmastime. This year he hired **seven guys** just to hang the lights and put up the decorations."

There were **sparkling lights** all over the house, the trees, and the bushes. There was **music blasting** from speakers on the roof. A plastic Santa popped up and down from the chimney. On the front lawn there was a giant sleigh pulled by a fleet of huge plastic reindeer, led by **Rudolph with a giant, glowing red nose**. And on the porch, a giant wooden soldier nutcracker stood guard.

"Wow!" George exclaimed. "This is awesome." He didn't like to compliment Louie, but he couldn't help himself.

"I know," Louie said.

"Why don't you let your parents know we're here?" Troop Leader Buttonwood suggested to Louie.

FARLEY FAMILY WINTER WONDERLAND

DON'T TOUCH!

George didn't really want to see Louie's mom. Mrs. Farley hated George because of how he'd **practically ruined** Louie's birthday party. Quickly, George hid behind Alex and Chris.

"Merry Christmas!" Louie's mom said as she came to her door. "My **Loo Loo Poo** told me you scouts would be coming by."

George started to laugh. *Loo Loo Poo* was funny. Then he stopped, because what was happening in the bottom of his belly was definitely *not* funny. **The super burp was back!**

Quickly, George tried to get Alex's attention. The boys had **a signal**: If George felt a burp coming, he was supposed to rub his belly and pat his head. Then Alex would get George out of the way.

Bing-bong. George rubbed his belly.

Ping-pong. He patted his head.

But Alex was busy staring at the lights in Louie's yard.

Bing-bong. George **rubbed** his belly harder.

Ping-pong. He **slammed** his head with his fist.

Finally, Alex turned and looked in George's direction.

It was too late. The burp escaped. And now it was ready to have a holly, jolly Christmas—right on Louie's front lawn!

"Dude! I'm sorry!" Alex shouted.

But George was already on Louie's porch, marching next to the wooden soldier. "Hup, two, three, four!" George's mouth shouted. "Hup, two, three, four."

"George, Beaver Scouts march when they're *hiking*, not decorating!" Troop Leader Buttonwood said.

But George kept marching.

"George! Stop acting weird at my house!" Louie shouted.

George wanted to stop acting weird. **He really did.** But he couldn't. George wasn't in charge anymore. George saluted the giant nutcracker. *Oops*. The nutcracker fell over and **one of its arms fell off**.

Troop Leader Buttonwood hurried toward the porch. "Ouch!" he shouted as he **whacked his head** on a big oak tree.

"Hey, who put that tree there?"

"That nutcracker is a valuable antique!" Louie's mother shouted. She reached out to grab the collar of George's coat.

George's feet hurried off the porch and raced across the lawn. His legs leaped on top of the giant Rudolph, and his tush started bouncing up and down. "Yahoo!" his mouth shouted. "Ride 'em, cowboy!"

"George Brown, get off that reindeer!" Louie's mother shouted. "Or I'll call the police!"

George's hands grabbed a long piece of tinsel off the sleigh and started **twirling it like a lasso** over his head. "Yee-haaaaa!" his mouth shouted out.

Rudolph **wobbled** from side to side. His red nose began to **flicker**. And then . . .

Pop! George felt the air rush right out of him. The super burp was gone.

Plop! Rudolph's nose fell off. There was **a loud crackling noise**, and all the lights on the Farley mansion went out.

"You broke the light circuit!" Louie's mother shouted at George. "It took seven men five days to put up these decorations. You **destroyed** them in one minute!"

George opened his mouth to say "I'm

sorry," and that's exactly what came out.

"Mrs. Farley, on behalf of the Beaver Scouts, I'm very sorry, too—" Troop Leader Buttonwood started to say.

But apparently **sorry wasn't good enough** for Mrs. Farley. "Get out of here!" she shouted to George.

George ran from Louie's front yard as fast as he could. There was no point in staying, anyway. George wasn't earning **a Good Neighbor badge** tonight. He'd be lucky if he wasn't **kicked out** of the troop.

Chapter 6

Mrs. Kelly was taking the Holiday Spectacular *really* seriously. So seriously that she'd insisted the kids **come to school on Saturday** for rehearsal. The show wasn't until Friday, so George didn't understand why there wasn't enough time to get it right during the school week. Mrs. Kelly was really **going nuts** over this thing.

Still, George headed off to Edith B. Sugarman Elementary School the minute he got out of work at Mr. Furstman's pet shop. That meant he had no free time at all today.

George had been in a **grumpy mood** since last night when Mrs. Farley called his parents to tell them what had happened to her Christmas decorations. George's mom and dad were so angry that they were making George give Mrs. Farley **all his money from his job at the pet shop** for the next two weeks to help pay to fix the giant wooden soldier and Rudolph. But that wasn't as bad as it could have been. If he had to pay it *all* back, he'd be working to **infinity**.

At least Alex was waiting on the steps of school when George arrived. "Hey, dude."

"Hey," George answered grumpily. "Do you believe we have to do this?"

Alex reached into his backpack and pulled out something wrapped in **gold foil**. "This will cheer you up," he told George. "Merry Christmas."

"Now? It's kind of early," George pointed out.

"After last night," Alex said, "I figured this couldn't wait."

George unwrapped the gift and stared at it strangely. **A bottle of mustard?** Huh? "Gee . . . um . . . thanks," George said.

"I read on a website that people use mustard to stop burps," Alex explained.

"Wow," George said. **"A burp cure for Christmas!** Just what I wanted. Thanks! I have something for you, too. I was saving it for Christmas Eve. But now is good, too."

George unzipped his backpack and pulled out a plastic bag filled with globs of pink, green, blue, and white already been chewed gum. "It's for your ABC gum ball," George told him. "I've been buying and chewing gum all month."

"Gee, thanks!" Alex said. "That's a great present." Alex was trying to get into the *Schminess Book of World Records* for **the biggest wad of chewed gum.**

George grinned. He was glad Alex liked his gift. He was also hoping that Alex's gift was the sure cure he'd been hoping for. Then Alex would be more than his best friend. **He'd be his hero.**

The boys went inside and took their seats in the auditorium. Since it was Saturday, Mrs. Kelly wasn't wearing her regular teacher clothes. She was wearing her normal person clothes. Well, normal for a person like Mrs. Kelly, anyway. Not too many people would wear a shirt with **dancing cats** all over it.

"All carolers go to the music room with Mrs. Cadenza," Mrs. Kelly announced. "Everyone else stay here with me. We'll work on your dance numbers."

Chris's hand shot up in the air. "I'm a bear. I don't dance or sing," Chris said. "Where should I go?"

Mrs. Kelly thought for a minute. "You can lie on the stage and **practice hibernating**."

"Okay," Chris said, standing up. "Sleeping onstage isn't as easy as it looks," he told George and Alex.

"We'll start with the snowflakes and the Winter Wonderland Watusi," Mrs. Kelly said. "I want to make sure you wiggle when you're supposed to."

George knew a lot about wiggling. And jiggling. And jumping. And bumping. Because that was what was going on inside his belly right now. **The super burp was back!**

Oh man. **This was *ba-a-ad*!** Mrs. Kelly never wanted any goofing around at her rehearsals.

Then he remembered that Alex's Christmas gift was in his backpack! Quickly, George unzipped his pack and began squirting **big, gooey globs of spicy mustard** down his throat.

"Whoa," George wheezed. "Spicy."

"What are you doing?" Sage asked.

George didn't answer. He just kept squeezing mustard into his mouth. His lips felt like **they were on fire**. His eyes were tearing, but . . .

Whoosh! Suddenly, George felt all the air rush out of him. The super burp was gone!

George's throat was on fire. He swore he could feel **smoke coming out**

of his ears. But none of that mattered because *the burp had gone up in smoke*!

Wahoo! Alex had found the cure for the super burp. It was a miracle! A scientific miracle! Alex was **a genius**!

When George got home from rehearsal, he was in the best mood ever. From now on, all he had to do was carry mustard everywhere he went. Mustard was his friend. He'd never have to be scared about burping again. He figured he'd eat **a whole bottle** right before the Holiday Spectacular, then no worries!

"George, there you are." His mother greeted him. "I have a surprise for you. I'm going to give you one of your Christmas presents early!"

George grinned. This day just kept getting better.

His mom handed him a green and red box.

Uh-oh, George thought as he opened the box. There it was: **the ugly Rudolph sweater** that had been hidden in the pile of dirty laundry.

"It's from Great-Aunt Catherine," George's mom said. "She knit it herself. She's coming over for dinner tonight. I thought she might like to see you in it."

"But it's got **a pom-pom** on it," George mumbled.

"I know," his mom said. "Isn't it cute?"

"It's too hot indoors to put on a sweater," George tried.

"I'll lower the heat," his mother answered.

And that was that. George was going to have to wear the ugly sweater. Well, fine. He'd do it tonight. But after that,

it was going in the bottom of his drawer,
never to be seen again.

"I knew you would love that sweater,
George," Great-Aunt Catherine said during
dinner that night. "Green is your color."

George looked down and poured some
more mustard on his pot roast.

"Mustard on pot roast?" his dad asked. "That's a new one."

"I like mustard on everything," George said. He poured some **on his mashed potatoes**, too.

"Since when?" his mother asked.

Since this afternoon when it squelched the belch, George thought to himself. But out loud he just said, "Is anyone else hot in here?" He pulled at the sweater and scratched his neck. **The wool was itchy.**

George's mom gave him a stern look. George went back to eating his mustard and pot roast.

"George is going to be a snowflake in the school play," his mom told Great-Aunt Catherine. "He's singing and dancing. What's the dance called again, George?"

"The Winter Wonderland Watusi,"

George grumbled. **He really hated that dance.**

"Isn't that lovely?" Great-Aunt Catherine said. "I bet he'll be as **cute as a button**."

George had no idea why Great-Aunt Catherine thought buttons were cute. And he didn't care.

"How is business at the store?" Great-Aunt Catherine asked George's mom.

George didn't hear his mom's answer. Some **funny business** was starting in his belly. There were bubbles bouncing around. Lots of them. Bing-bong. Ping-pong. Bing-bang. Ping-pang.

But George wasn't worried. He had *the cure*! He picked up the bottle of mustard and started pouring it down his throat.

The mustard **burned**. But the bubbles didn't stop. They just bounced harder and faster.

The mustard made George's eyes
tear up and his nose run. The bubbles
were running, too. Right up into George's
mouth, over his tongue, around his teeth,
and . . .

Everyone at the table—his mom, his
dad, and Great-Aunt Catherine—stared
at George. He opened his mouth to say
"Excuse me." But that's not what came
out. Instead, he shouted, *"Everybody,
Watusi!"*

George's feet jumped up. His
tush started to wiggle all around. His
shoulders started to shake. Then his
whole body began to spin around and
around **like a snowflake in the wind**.

A thread from George's sweater got caught on the back of his chair. George didn't realize it, but the more he spun around, the more the sweater **unraveled**.

"Wa-Wa-Watusi!" George's mouth shouted. "Join in, folks!"

"Oh, George!" His mother had both hands over her face.

"Soldier, take your seat," his dad ordered.

But the super burp didn't take orders from anyone. It *gave* orders. And right now it was ordering George's body to spin harder—**which made the yarn unravel faster**.

"The sweater!" Great-Aunt Catherine shouted.

"Watusi!" George's mouth shouted back. His rear end wiggled. And then . . .

Whoosh! George felt the air rush out of him as if something had popped in the bottom of his belly. The super burp was gone, and George was standing in the middle of what used to be the ugly Christmas sweater. Now there was a big pile of yarn and a bright red pom-pom.

"Son, what did you think you were doing?" George's dad demanded.

George looked down at the pile of wool. "Um . . . the Watusi?" George said quietly. He reached down and picked up

Rudolph's red nose. "At least the pom-pom's still good," he added hopefully.

George spent the rest of the night in his room. He was sorry that Great-Aunt Catherine had been so upset. Yet in some ways, the super burp had actually done him **a favor**. He'd never have to wear that ugly sweater again. And it turned out that he was really **amazing at the Watusi**. He hoped he'd be as good for the holiday play . . . but without the burp, of course!

Chapter 7

"Well, the mustard worked once," Alex said.

"Once is not enough, I'm afraid," George said as he and Alex waited backstage with the other fourth-graders on Friday afternoon. The Holiday Spectacular was going to start **any minute now**. "But I've been burp-free since then. So I figure maybe the burp is already on winter vacation."

Alex didn't look so sure.

"I brought lots of stuff **in case of an emergency**," George continued as he opened his backpack so Alex could see all the things he had inside. There was mustard to burn the burp, a rolling pin to roll the bubbles out of his body, a brown paper bag to blow all that extra air into, and a bottle of water to drown the bubbles.

"One of these just has to work," George said. This show was dumb enough as it was. **The last thing it needed was a surprise guest performance by the super burp.**

"We're about to start," Mrs. Kelly told everyone.

Louie had his guitar. He stared at George's white, glittery snowflake costume and **started laughing**. "You look beautiful," Louie teased.

George didn't answer. He knew he looked ridiculous, **especially next to Louie**, who wore jeans, a black leather jacket, and dark sunglasses.

"Good luck!" Mrs. Kelly called out. She looked really stressed out. As she pulled a tissue out of her sleeve and raised her arm to wipe the **globs of sweat** from her forehead, George could see a big, wet pit stain on her shirt.

George was glad the snowflake dance was first. That way he'd get it over with quickly.

"Chris, when you're onstage, curl up in a ball," Mrs. Kelly said. "Don't move around. Remember, you're hibernating."

"Don't worry," Chris answered as he pulled on his bear mask. "I've been practicing. Yesterday I took a two-hour nap, and it went perfectly."

Once Chris took his place onstage, the curtain rose.

George started to feel something weird in his stomach. There was no binging or bonging. It felt more like

hundreds of centipedes crawling around his insides. Oh no! He couldn't burp now.

George waited in fear for the centipedes to crawl up into his throat. But it didn't happen. The creepy-crawlies stayed in his belly. This wasn't the super burp. It was good old normal stage fright. Not that stage fright was so wonderful, either.

"Come on, Georgie," Sage whispered as the music started. "That's the cue for the snowflakes." She smoothed her costume and pulled at his arm.

George walked onstage behind her. He looked out into the audience. There

were his parents, Principal McKeon, and the kids and teachers from all the other grades. It felt like they were all staring at him, **daring him to mess up**. George just stood there, a snowflake frozen with fear. He couldn't dance. He couldn't even move.

The music started up.

"Georgie, come on," Sage insisted. **"Wiggle your Watusi."**

George started to laugh, which helped him relax. A second later he was dancing the Watusi and singing with the other

snowflakes. He pretended to be floating just like Mrs. Kelly had told them to. He spun Sage around in a circle—and didn't once stick his tongue out at her, even though she was doing that **weird blinking-her-eyes thing** whenever she looked at him. At the end he lay down on the ground like he was part of a blanket of snow. *"Snow is falling everywhere, snowflakes flying in the air. Landing softly on a branch, dancing a lovely snowflake dance."*

George ran off the stage as soon as the song was over. *Phew.* He'd made it through—**and without a burp**. The nightmare was over. He started to pull the glittery snowflake costume over his head.

"No, George, you have to leave that on for the final bow," Mrs. Kelly reminded him.

Bummer.

As Max and Mike went onstage with Julianna to sing their "Happy Elves" song, Louie walked over to George. "At least you didn't **freak out** like you did at the talent show," Louie said.

Was Louie ever going to let him forget that? **So what if George had dive-bombed into the principal's arms during the performance?** Was he the only kid in the world who ever did that?

Actually, he probably was.

"You're next," Mrs. Kelly told Louie. Her hair was stuck to her forehead with sweat.

"See you later, *Snowflake*," Louie said to George. Then he headed off onto the stage.

"You know, when I blow, winter's here," Louie sang as he played his guitar onstage. *"I'm a cold, cold wind. Gonna blow the snow, whoa, whoa, whoa!"*

Suddenly, George felt as if a wind were blowing in the bottom of his belly. The wind was **whooshing bubbles** all up through his chest and around the red thing hanging down in the back of his throat.

George leaped toward his backpack. He needed his mustard or the rolling pin or the bottle of water. But there was no time . . .

Bubble, bubble. **George was in trouble.**

Big trouble. Because suddenly, George's feet ran onstage and started dancing—right in the middle of Louie's solo!

Louie glared at George.

"George, get off the stage!" Mrs. Kelly hissed from behind the curtain.

George wanted to get off. But the burp wouldn't let him. His body started spinning around in circles like a snowflake being blown around in a blizzard. A few people in the audience giggled. Some started clapping.

Louie's face turned bright red. He was really mad. But he kept on singing. *"I send chills down your spine, blow needles off the pine . . ."*

George spun faster and faster. More people laughed. They thought it was part of the act.

Bash! George spun right into Louie.

Crash! Louie fell to the floor.

The audience laughed harder.

"I'm going to get you, *Snowflake!*" Louie shouted as he scrambled to his feet and ran toward George.

George's feet took off running. Louie chased after him. The audience cheered.

"Snowflakes, go out there," Mrs. Kelly shouted to the kids who had gathered backstage to watch what was going on. "Do your dance again. Do anything. Just distract the audience."

Whoosh! Just then, George felt a blast of air rush out of him. It was like someone had popped a balloon in his belly. The super burp was gone. But Louie was still there. **And he looked mad enough to knock George clear to the North Pole.**

George had to do something!

"See, your song made a blizzard," he said, pointing to the dancing snowflakes. The audience cheered louder.

Louie stopped chasing George. He smiled at the audience and took a bow.

A few minutes later, the curtain had come down, and the show was over. **But Louie was still angry**. "You did it again, George."

"Why are you mad?" George asked. "We got more applause than anybody."

Louie thought about that. "You mean *I* did," he said finally. "It was *my* song!"

"Okay, okay," George said. Then he ran back into the boys' room to get out of that costume as fast as he could. George didn't want to think about the Holiday Spectacular **ever again**. After

all, there were more important things
to think about. Like how tomorrow was
Christmas Eve. That meant presents,
good food, and best of all, *no more school
for two weeks.*

Talk about *spectacular*!

Chapter 8

"Is it time?" George asked his parents excitedly. There was a huge pile of presents beneath the tree. **Every year, George got one gift on Christmas Eve.** He had to wait for Christmas morning to open the others.

George's dad smiled. "I guess by twenty-one hours, it's officially Christmas Eve," he said, reaching under the tree. "How about I give Mom her gift first?"

George's mouth didn't say a word.

But his face must have said a lot because his parents **started to laugh**. His mom reached under the tree and then handed George the first box.

"Thanks," George said as he tore the paper off and opened the box as fast as he could.

Weird. The box was completely empty except for **a small photograph of George and Kevin Camilleri**, George's best friend back when he'd lived in Cherrydale.

"What's this?" George asked his parents.

"That's your gift," his mom explained.

Huh?

"We're giving you Kevin for Christmas," George's dad explained. "He's flying into town on December 26 and staying until New Year's."

"Awesome!" George exclaimed. "This is an amazing gift!"

George was really happy. It was starting out as a great Christmas! And with Kevin around, New Year's Eve would be even better. Unless, of course, the new year brought new burps. **Then there might be trouble.** *Bubble* trouble. And George had no idea how he'd ever explain *that* to Kevin.

BEAVER BROOK
PRESS GAZETTE

Chapter 1

"What time is it now?" George asked his mother for about **the gazillionth time** on Monday morning. It seemed like they'd been waiting at the airport forever, but there was still no Kevin Camilleri in sight.

"It's three minutes later than the last time you asked." George's mom laughed. "His flight will be here soon. Hang in there."

George was tired of hanging in there. He'd been hanging in there since last night when his parents made him go to bed at his regular bedtime even though it was still Christmas and he was too excited to sleep.

George was a little nervous about

seeing **his old best friend**. He wondered
if Kevin had changed. Did he still eat
tomatoes all the time? Was he still into
karate? And the really big question—**was
George still his best friend?**

George still thought of Kevin as his
best friend, even though he had another
best friend, too—Alex. George just figured
Kevin was his Cherrydale best friend, and
Alex was his Beaver Brook one.

Zip. Zip. Zip. George slid the zipper
on his new leather jacket up and down.
He loved that sound. He pulled it fast.
Zip, zip, zip. He pulled it slowly. *Ziiiip.*
Ziiiip.

"George, stop," his mother scolded.
"You're going to ruin your new jacket.
And you've only had it since yesterday."

That was true. The jacket had been
waiting for George under the tree on
Christmas morning. **He'd been wanting**

it for months! And that wasn't the only awesome gift George had gotten. His uncle had sent him the new *Caveman Battle 2* video game. George only got to play the game two times yesterday, which was a bummer because he had wanted to get really good at it before Kevin came.

Zip. Ziiiiiip. Zip.

"There he is!" George's mother shouted suddenly.

Sure enough, **there was Kevin**, walking toward them with a flight attendant.

"GEORGEROONIO!" Kevin shouted.

"KEVSTER!" George shouted back. He raced over to his buddy. "I can't believe you're here."

"Me neither," Kevin said.

"It's good to see you, Kevin," George's mom said as she signed a form the flight attendant had handed her.

"Let's get your luggage."

"Okay," Kevin said. "I checked one bag. But I carried my *important* stuff on the plane in this backpack." He patted it.

"What do you have in there?" George asked.

"Nothing *now*," Kevin told him. "It *was* **filled with tomatoes**. But I ate them all on the way here."

George grinned. Same old Kevin.

The boys followed George's mom to the luggage carousel. The belt was moving, and there were already a few pieces of luggage traveling around and around.

"I hope mine didn't get lost," Kevin said. "That happened once."

"I'm sure there's nothing to worry about," George's mother assured him.

But she was wrong. There *was* something to worry about. George had just started feeling something big and bubbly taking a trip up his belly.

The super burp was back! And from the way those bubbles felt, it was ready to burst out any minute. The bubbles galloped on George's gallbladder. They circled his spleen. They **trampled over** his tongue. George shoved his fist into his mouth and tried to punch the bubbles back down where they belonged.

"George, get your fingers out of your mouth," his mother said. She pulled his arm by the elbow.

And then . . .

The megapowerful super burp escaped. It was so loud that pilots flying at thirty thousand feet must have heard it.

"Awesome!" Kevin cheered.

"George, what do you say?" his mother asked.

George opened his mouth to say "Excuse me." But that's not what came out. Instead, George's mouth announced, "Ride the carousel!" **His rear end plopped itself down on the luggage carousel.** Now George was riding around with the luggage.

"George!" his mother exclaimed. "Get off there this instant!"

George *wanted* to get off. But he wasn't in charge anymore. The super burp was. George's hands grabbed a pink polka-dotted bag that was circling on the luggage carousel. He couldn't help himself.

Kevin was **doubled over**, he was laughing so hard.

"Whose is this?" George's mouth shouted.

"Mine!" a girl in a green and yellow jacket told him.

"Here ya go!" George's mouth said. His hands tossed her the bag. Then he picked up a black bag with a big red ribbon on the handle.

"That one's mine," a woman in a gray overcoat said. George's hands threw the bag to her.

"Thanks," the woman told him. "I've never been to an airport with luggage service before."

"Yo, Georgeroonio!" Kevin called to him. "The red suitcase is mine."

George grabbed the bag and tossed it to Kevin. **Soon bags were flying everywhere.**

"Can you get my green bag next?" a teenager in a hooded sweatshirt asked.

"Sure thing!" George's mouth exclaimed. His legs started to run for the green bag.

"Hey, kid! Get off of there!"
a security guard shouted out
suddenly. He leaped onto the
luggage carousel and started
chasing George. George's feet
began to run. His legs hopped
over bags on the moving
luggage carousel.

"Oomf!" The security
guard groaned as he tripped
over a huge black suitcase with
wheels.

"Hey, watch it!" a man shouted. "I've
got my camera in there!"

"Sorry," the security guard apologized.
He scrambled to his feet.

George's feet kept running. And
then . . .

Whoosh! George felt all the air
rush right out of him. It was as though
someone had popped a giant balloon in

the bottom of his belly. **The super burp was gone.** But George was still on the luggage carousel. He leaped off before he could get in any more trouble.

"That was hilarious!" Kevin exclaimed, running over to George. "You haven't changed. **You're still clowning around.**"

George hadn't meant to clown around. But how was he supposed to explain the super burp to Kevin, the

guard, or his mother? He looked up at the guard and opened his mouth to say "I'm sorry." And that's exactly what came out.

"You're going to have to take that troublemaker out of here," the security guard told George's mother.

George frowned. **Troublemaker?** More like *bubble* maker. Of course, that was pretty much the same thing.

Chapter 2

"You're here for a whole week!" George said excitedly as Kevin unpacked his things.

"Yeah, I was so psyched when I found out that the regional karate tournament was in Beaver Brook," Kevin said.

"What?" George asked.

"Didn't your mom tell you? There's going to be **a big karate tournament** at the Beaver Brook martial arts center on Wednesday." Kevin pulled a white karate uniform out of his bag along with a bright green cloth belt.

"Whoa! **You're a green belt?**" George asked.

Kevin nodded proudly. "I earned it last month. I'm going to be **competing against other green belts** in the sparring and board-breaking competitions. You're gonna come and watch, right?"

"Definitely," George said.

Just then, the phone rang.

"George, it's Alex," his mom called up to him.

"Who's Alex?" Kevin asked.

"My friend," George said. "I wrote to you about him."

"He's not the rich kid with the sneakers that have wheels, is he? The mean guy who plays guitar?" Kevin asked.

"No, that's Louie," George said. "He's *not* my friend. Alex is the **really smart** guy."

"Oh," Kevin said. "Yeah. I remember you writing about him."

"Be right back," George told Kevin as he hurried into the hall to the phone.

"Hey, Alex," George said.

"Dude, you wanna come to the skating rink with Chris and me?" Alex asked.

"Um . . . sure," George said. "Let me just check with Kevin."

"Who's Kevin?"

"My best friend from Cherrydale," George explained. "I told you about him. The guy who loves tomatoes. He's visiting. **Isn't that cool?**"

"Uh . . . sure, I guess," Alex said. "Did he bring ice skates with him?"

"He can always rent a pair," George replied.

"Maybe he's tired from flying," Alex said. "He might want to take a nap or something."

"Nah, he's wide awake," George said. "I'm sure he'll want to come."

"Oh, okay," Alex said. "Then Chris and I will meet you *both* there."

That was weird, George thought as he hung up the phone. It almost sounded **like Alex didn't want to meet Kevin**.

Nah. He was probably just imagining it.

"This is a pretty small rink," Kevin said later that afternoon as he and George laced up their skates.

"Yeah," George agreed. "But there's a great café. They serve these cheese fries that are **the best ever**."

"There are cheese fries at the pizzeria in the Cherrydale Mall now," Kevin told George. "They're covered in mozzarella cheese and tomato sauce. Jeremy, Kadeem, and I split an order last week. None of us could eat the whole thing by ourselves. It's huge."

Hearing about the guys from his old school **made George feel homesick** for Cherrydale.

Just then, Alex skated over to greet them. "Yo, dude, hurry up and get on the ice," Alex said. "We're gonna make a train. You don't want to be **the caboose**." Alex paused for a minute and looked at Kevin. "Oh, hi," he added.

"This is Kevin," George said. "Kevin, this is Alex."

"Hey," Kevin said.

The two boys stared at each other.

"Okay," George said finally, breaking the silence. "Let's go, Kevster."

"Um . . . we move pretty fast when we skate in a train," Alex told Kevin. "I'm just warning you."

"That's all right," Kevin said. "I skate fast." The boys all skated over to where some of George's other friends were already starting to go around the ice.

Julianna was at the head of the train. Chris was holding on to her, Alex was holding on to Chris, George was holding on to Alex, and Kevin was holding on to George. **That made Kevin the caboose.**

"Okay, we're going around the turn," Julianna called back to the other kids.

"Wahooooo!" George shouted as the train of skaters went around the rink.

"Awesome!" Kevin cheered.

By the time the train broke up, George was totally out of breath. But Kevin seemed fine. In fact, he was talking a mile a minute.

"You remember that time we all did a backward train, and **Suzanne landed on her rear end**?" Kevin said. "Man, was she mad."

George started to laugh.

"Who's Suzanne?" Alex asked.

"She's this girl in Cherrydale," George said.

"There are no words to describe Suzanne," Kevin said. **He and George**

laughed harder.

"Whatever."
Alex rolled
his eyes. "I'm
going to skate
with Julianna,"
he said. "You
coming, Chris?"

"Sure,"
Chris said. He
turned to Kevin.
"See you around."

George watched as the two boys skated off. **Alex was sure acting weird today.** He couldn't figure out what it was all about. Then, the very next moment, he heard a horrible sound—a screeching noise so annoying, it made his hair stand on end.

"Oh, *Georgie!*" Sage cried out. "There you are!"

Kevin gave George a look. *"Georgie?"* he repeated.

George shook his head. "Don't ask."

"I've been waiting to show you my new skating skirt. I got it for Christmas," Sage said **as she twirled around**. Then she smiled at Kevin. "Aren't you going to introduce me to your friend, *Georgie?*"

"Kevin, this is Sage," George said.

"You're Georgie's friend from his old school," Sage said. "Alex said you were coming to the rink. I'm glad you're here.

I want to know all about what Georgie was like when he lived in Cherrydale."

"He wasn't any different," Kevin said.

But that wasn't true. Not at all. Ever since he moved to Beaver Brook, there was something *very* different about George: **the magic burps**. And right now one was bouncing around in the bottom of his belly! There were hundreds of tiny bubbles that ping-ponged their way into his chest and bing-bonged their way up into his throat. And then . . .

"Whoa! Nice, Georgeroonio!" Kevin exclaimed.

There were lots of words to describe the magical super burp, but *nice* wasn't

one of them. *Crazy* was a better word. And that's what the super burp wanted to do. Go *craaaazzzyyyy!*

George's feet began spinning him in a circle on the ice. His arms shot up in the air like a figure skater. It was as though George were an old-fashioned puppet, and **someone else was pulling the strings**.

George's leg stuck itself out behind him, like he was a ballerina on ice. Then he began to skate backward.

"Watch out, everyone!" Louie shouted as he skated out of George's way. "Weirdo freak on skates coming through."

George began to twirl on the ice. Skaters dashed right and left, trying to get

out of his way. No
one wanted to be
knocked over by a
whirling, twirling
tornado on ice.
George's feet
jumped up in the air.
His body began to spin in a
double axel.

Unfortunately, George didn't know
how to do a double axel. Neither did the
super burp. **But that didn't stop it from
trying!**

Thud! George landed
right on his rear end
and slid across the
ice.

THUD!

Then he hopped back up onto his feet and started dancing around the rink—in the wrong direction.

"Hey! Watch where you're skating," one guy shouted.

"You almost bashed into me," his friend added.

"Dude, I'm coming!" Alex started skating toward George.

George's hands reached out and grabbed Sage by the hand. **He spun her around on the ice.**

"Oh, Georgie!" she squealed. "We're skating doubles! It's like the Olympics!"

Whoosh! Suddenly it felt as though someone had taken a pin and popped a balloon right in the middle of George's belly. The super burp was gone. But George was still there—**holding Sage's hand**.

George dropped her hand fast.

"That was awesome, Georgeroonio," Kevin said as he skated over. "Wait until I tell the guys at home."

Alex frowned and looked sadly at George. "That was a big one," he said in a low voice. "Sorry I couldn't get over to you in time."

George nodded.

A skating instructor in an orange vest glided over to the boys. "Kid, you can't go flying around the ice like that," he told George. "You're **banned from the ice** for the rest of the day."

George didn't argue with him. After all, he *had* gone flying around on the ice. Everyone had seen him. What they didn't see was *why*. A magical super burp wasn't something you could see. It wasn't even something you would believe existed—unless, of course, you were the one burping it.

Chapter 3

"You don't have to get off the ice, too," George said as he and Alex took off their skates and headed over to the café. "I'm okay hanging here by myself." He sat down at a table and **looked out at the ice**. Kevin was skating around in circles by himself.

"It's all right," Alex said, taking the seat across the table. "I can look for some more ABC gum. You wouldn't believe how many people stick their gum under tabletops once it loses its flavor." Alex reached under one of the tables and pulled off **a glob of green gum**. "This is a fresh one," he said. "Still gooey."

"That glob puts you one piece of gum closer to being in the *Schminess Book of World Records*," George told him.

"Hey, I almost forgot to tell you," Alex said. "There's a traveling *Schminess Book of World Records* show. It's coming to Beaver Brook for one day. There will be lots of creepy stuff . . . **the longest fingernail in the world**, a potato that looks like Elvis Presley, and of course, there's the current world's largest gum ball. It belongs to some guy from Alaska. I definitely want to see that."

"Totally," George agreed.

"I'm going to talk to the *Schminess* people there about entering my gum ball," Alex continued. "I'm nervous, but I think I should do it."

"Well, I can go," George said. "You wouldn't be so nervous if you knew you had a friend with you. And I bet Kevin would go, too."

Alex didn't answer for a moment. Then he said, "Yeah . . . I guess that'd be okay. It's Wednesday afternoon."

"Sure . . ." George began. Then he stopped himself. **Wednesday was the day of Kevin's karate championship.** "Uh-oh!"

"What? Is that a problem?" Alex asked.

Oh yeah, George thought. But this ABC gum ball was really important to Alex. He couldn't let him down. He was his best pal in Beaver Brook.

Before George could say another word, some of the other kids came into the café.

"I'm starved," Julianna said, heading over to the counter.

Louie said, "I'm in the mood for a hoagie."

"I want a hoagie, too," Max said.

"Exactly like Louie's."

"That's what *I* was going to say," Mike told Max. "How come you always copy me?"

"Georgie, you want to share cheese fries?" Sage asked. "You can have most of them."

"Nah," George said.

Kevin walked up to the lady at the counter. Her name tag said STELLA. "Can I just get some tomatoes?" he asked.

"Sorry, kid," Stella said. "We only serve tomatoes on a hamburger."

Kevin thought about that for a minute. "Well, then give me a hamburger with **extra tomatoes**, please," he said.

"Okay, we can do that," Stella said. She wrote the order on her pad.

"But hold the mustard and the ketchup," Kevin said. "Hold the bun, too. And hold the hamburger."

Stella looked down at her pad. "But that only leaves the extra tomatoes."

Kevin gave her a big smile. "Exactly."

"I once saw Kevin eat **three pints of cherry tomatoes** for supper," George told the kids.

"And for dessert I had a massive beefsteak tomato," Kevin boasted.

"Didn't **all that citric acid** give you diarrhea?" Alex asked him.

"All that what?" Kevin asked.

"Citric acid," Alex said. "That's what's in tomatoes. It can give you the runs."

"Sounds like a good enemy for Toiletman," Chris said with a laugh.

"For *who*?" Kevin asked.

"Toiletman," George repeated. "He's a superhero Chris made up."

"Oh." Kevin laughed. He turned to Alex. "My stomach is like iron. I'm the **champion tomato eater** of Cherrydale Elementary School!"

"Yeah?" Alex said. "Well, I'm going to be a *world* champion soon. I've been collecting ABC gum, and soon I'll have the world's largest gum ball in the universe."

TOILETMAN

"So it's not the biggest yet?" Kevin asked him.

Alex shook his head. "But I'm entering it in next year's record book. There's a *Schminess* show here on—"

"Hey, whose turn is it to order food?" George interrupted. He wanted to change the subject before Alex announced that **the *Schminess* show was the same day as Kevin's karate tournament**.

"What are you having?" Kevin asked George. "It's my treat!"

The truth was George wasn't hungry at all. Tomatoes weren't the only thing that could give a guy a bellyache. Having to choose between your two best friends could make you pretty sick to your stomach, too.

Chapter 4

"Take that, Cave Dweller," Kevin shouted later that day as he clicked the button on his video game controller. The caveman on the screen picked up his club and **smashed** the other guy on the head.

"You've destroyed another one of my guys!" George groaned. "I have only two left in my whole tribe. Are you sure you haven't played this game before?"

"Never," Kevin insisted. "Watch out! Here comes another **avalanche of boulders**." He clicked a button on the control pad, and his caveman leaped over them.

Just then, the phone rang.

"George, it's Alex," George's dad shouted a moment later. "He says it's important."

"Call him back later," Kevin said. "You can talk to Alex any time. I'm only here for a few days."

"Oh, come on," George said. "I'll make it fast and come right back."

"Then *I* can go back to destroying you," Kevin said with a grin.

"Whatever." George went into the hall and picked up the phone. "Hey, Alex," he said.

"Hey, dude," Alex replied. "That was one bad burp this afternoon at the rink."

"Yeah," George agreed.

"But listen to what I found on this new website. It's called **The Burp No More Blog**," Alex said excitedly. "*Marshmallows* can cure burps."

"Marshmallows?" George asked.

"Uh-huh," Alex said. "They're sticky, so when you eat them they kind of **glue the bubbles together** into  one giant bubble that's too big to move out of your stomach! If the bubble can't leave your stomach, it can't be burped."

That made sense. **And marshmallows tasted a whole lot better than mustard.** George hung up the phone and went back to his room. "Kevin," he said. "I think it's hot cocoa time."

Kevin looked at him strangely. "I thought we were going to finish this game."

"We can do that later," George told him. "Right now, I want some cocoa . . . *with lots of marshmallows.*"

"What are you trying to do?" Kevin asked as he watched George pour half a bag of mini marshmallows into his mug. George added a few more marshmallows and then splashed a little hot cocoa on top of them.

"You have cocoa your way, and I'll have it mine," George said. Then he took a sip. Only he couldn't really sip; he mostly chewed the marshmallows.

Kevin stared at him. "Does that taste good?" he asked.

George didn't hear a word Kevin said. He couldn't. Kevin's voice was drowned out by **the band of bubbles playing in his belly**. There were bing-bangs and ping-pangs. Then bing-bongs and cling-clangs.

The super burp was back!

Quickly, George slurped up another huge mouthful of marshmallows, trying to stick those bubbles together. But the bubbles fought back, bouncing harder than ever inside him.

And then . . .

B·U·U·U·R·P!

George let out a chocolate-marshmallow-flavored super burp. It was only a miniburp, but it was still *magic.* The next thing George knew, his fingers started grabbing marshmallows from the bag and **shoving them up his nose**.

Kevin started laughing. "You crack me up."

George's fingers shoved a few more mini marshmallows up his nostrils. Then his nose got into the act and let out **a humongous sneeze**.

"*Achooo!*" Ooey, gooey white marshmallow shot out across the kitchen.

"Gross!" Kevin shouted. "But in a good way," he added with a laugh.

"*Achoo!*" George's nose sneezed again. More flew out.

Whoosh! Just then, George felt something pop in the bottom of his belly. All the air rushed out of him. The super burp was gone. But there were still mini marshmallows up his nose. George poked his little finger into his nostril and pulled them out.

Kevin laughed so hard, **hot chocolate came out of *his* nose**. "Hilarious, Georgeroonio," he said.

But George didn't think it was hilarious. He thought it was awful. How many burps could a guy take in one day, anyway?

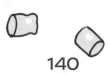

Chapter 5

The next morning, George and Kevin woke to the sound of the vacuum cleaner. They went downstairs to find George's mom cleaning the living room.

"Make your own breakfast," she told them. "I have too much to do before our New Year's Eve party. I'm running around like **a chicken without a head today**."

George cracked up. The idea of a headless chicken wearing his mother's bathrobe and slippers and vacuuming the living room rug was hilarious. But his mom wasn't in the mood to laugh. So George shut his mouth and walked toward the kitchen.

"Is it just going to be a bunch of grown-ups and us at this party?" Kevin asked George.

"Nope," George said. "I invited Alex, too."

"Oh." Kevin didn't sound too happy about that.

"Alex is a good guy," George said.

"It wasn't nice **the way he bragged** about maybe getting in the *Schminess Book of World Records*," Kevin said.

George thought about mentioning that Kevin had been **bragging about eating tomatoes**, too. But what would be the point?

"After breakfast, I have to practice my karate," Kevin said as he poured himself a bowl of Crunchy Munchies. "The tournament is **tomorrow afternoon**."

"Don't remind me," George mumbled

as he shoved a spoonful of Wheat Wonkers into his mouth.

"What?" Kevin asked.

George swallowed his cereal. "I . . . um . . . said, 'You don't need to remind me,'" George fibbed. "Because . . . um . . . **what kind of a guy would I be if I forgot about your karate tournament?**"

A guy with one less best friend, George thought quietly to himself. Because no matter which friend he went with, come Wednesday, that was exactly the kind of guy he was going to be.

Later that morning before George's mom left for work, she warned him. "Your dad came in late from the base last night, so he's taking a nap. Please don't wake him. **And whatever you do, don't make a mess.**"

"We won't," George promised.

"Okay, so what do we do now?" Kevin asked.

"You want to play video games?" George suggested.

"Nah," Kevin said. "I'm played out."

The boys sat there, trying to come up with **a plan that wasn't noisy or messy**.

"I'm hungry," Kevin said finally.

"But we just finished breakfast," George said.

"I know," Kevin said. "But I can always eat. You got any tomatoes?"

"I think there's a few left," George said.

"Cool," Kevin told him. "Maybe we could chop them up with some marshmallows, since you like them so much."

George thought about that. The super burp had been **a small one**. Maybe the marshmallows had helped a little. It was possible that the more he ate, the less he'd burp.

"And then top the whole thing off with chocolate syrup," Kevin continued. **"A chocolate, marshmallow, and tomato parfait!"**

George wasn't sure what that would taste like. But he figured it would be fun to make. He went to the refrigerator and pulled out the tomatoes. Then he took the chocolate syrup and the marshmallows from the cupboard.

"I'll chop the tomatoes while you mix the marshmallows and the chocolate syrup," Kevin said.

George nodded and poured what was left of the marshmallows into a big bowl. Then he squeezed the chocolate syrup container. **But nothing happened.**

"I can't get the chocolate out," George said.

"Squeeze harder," Kevin said. "Here. Let me try."

Kevin took the bottle, squeezed, and . . . *Squirt!* Chocolate syrup **flew out of the bottle**. It was like all the chocolate in the bottle came out in one giant glob. But instead of landing in the mixing bowl, **thick, gooey syrup splattered all over the floor, the counter, and the clean tablecloth** George's mom had put out that morning.

Uh-oh! "My mom will kill us if she sees this," George said.

"I'm so sorry!" Kevin said. "We'll clean up fast and just stick the tablecloth in the washing machine."

"Do you know how to use a washing machine?" George asked him.

Kevin shook his head.

"Me neither. And we can't wake up my dad," George reminded Kevin. He looked around the kitchen.

"How hard could it be to run a washing machine?" Kevin said as he gathered up the tablecloth and headed for the laundry room.

"How much soap do you think we should put in?" George asked Kevin a few minutes later as they stuffed the tablecloth into the washer.

"Lots," Kevin said. "It's pretty dirty."

"Yeah." George poured in more soap. "I think half the box should do it." He closed the lid and pressed the button that read WASH. Immediately, water began to pour into the machine.

"We did it!" Kevin cheered.

"Now let's go clean up the rest of the mess," George said.

They were wiping down the counters and floor when George and Kevin heard some **weird clunking noises** coming from the laundry room.

"Does your washer always sound like that?" Kevin asked.

George shook his head.

"Uh-oh!" Kevin screamed and pointed.

The laundry room was knee-deep in a sea of soap bubbles!

"This is *ba-a-ad*!" George cried out.

"Maybe we put in too much detergent," Kevin said.

"Gee, you think?" George asked him angrily.

"Don't get mad at me," Kevin said. "*You* poured it in."

"Yeah, but *you* told me to put in a lot," George pointed out. **He shook his head.** "It doesn't matter. I have to turn this thing off." He walked toward the machine.

"Whoa!" he exclaimed as he slipped and fell.

At the same time, Kevin slipped and landed on top of George.

George scrambled out from under Kevin and tried to crawl to the machine. "Which do you think is the off button?"

"I don't see it," Kevin answered. "Just pull the plug."

"I can't *find* the plug," George said.

"WHAT'S GOING ON IN HERE?"

George turned around at the sound of his dad's booming voice.

"We . . . uh . . . we got chocolate sauce on mom's tablecloth, and we knew she'd be mad, and so we tried to wash it, and . . ." George stopped midsentence. The rest was pretty easy to figure out.

George's dad was shaking his head as he turned off the washer. But when he spoke, he didn't sound so mad. "Come on, soldiers. We have to get this cleaned up before the water soaks through to the basement. George, you go upstairs and get some towels. Kevin and I will start mopping."

"I'm sorry we woke you, Dad," George said as he headed upstairs.

"I actually wish you'd woken me up *before* you tried to do the laundry," his dad said. "Now get moving and find those towels. This cleanup is going to take a while."

Oh man. **Even without a burp, George just couldn't get away from bubble trouble.**

Chapter 6

"Is this hill as good as the one behind our school in Cherrydale?" Kevin asked George as the boys dragged George's sled a few blocks to Jumping Mouse Lane. George's dad had ordered them out of the house after they'd cleaned the kitchen and the laundry room. He said it was probably **safer that way**.

"This hill's awesome," George promised Kevin. "There aren't any trees, so you're not always smashing into things on the way down."

There were plenty of kids on the hill when the boys arrived. Julianna was

zipping down on a red sled. Chris and Alex were right behind her. Max and Mike were busy dragging Louie up the hill on **a shiny metal disk** that must have been a Christmas present. Sage was busy making snow angels.

"You mind if I go first?" Kevin asked.

"Go ahead," George said.

"I'll bring your sled right back so you can have a turn," Kevin told him.

As Kevin started whizzing down the hill, Alex came trudging up, pulling his sled. "Have you tried eating marshmallows yet?" he asked.

"Yeah," George said. "They didn't exactly work. **I'm beginning to think there is no cure for a super burp.**"

"There's a cure for everything," Alex told him. "Sometimes scientists take decades, even centuries, to find cures. But they find them eventually."

George frowned. *Decades? Centuries? Eventually?*

"I need help now, Alex," George said. He stopped speaking for a moment. "Actually, I need help *right now!*" Because at just that moment, something was brewing in the bottom of George's belly. Something bing-bongy and ping-pongy.

Couldn't the burp give George even one afternoon off?

Bing-bong! Ping-pong! Apparently not.

Alex looked at George. "Oh, dude, not again!" he said.

George nodded. But this time the burp wasn't going to escape. George was going to get that burp to go in reverse! He dropped to his knees and began to roll down the hill. First his head was up. Then his feet. Then his head. The burp was getting more and more confused. It didn't know which end was up.

George rolled **faster and faster** through the cold snow. Feet. Head. Feet. Head. Up. Down. Up . . .

Whoosh! Suddenly, George felt all the air rush out of him. It was like someone popped a balloon in the bottom of his belly. Hooray!

George stood and raised his fist in the air. *Victory!* Cold, wet snow was in his hair, on his face, under his collar, and all over his coat and pants. **Even his tighty whities were cold and wet.** But it was worth it.

"Look, Daddy!" a little boy shouted, pointing to George. "It's Frosty." He began to sing. *"Frosty the Snowman was a jolly, happy soul . . ."*

George was jolly and happy, all right. He'd just squelched a belch!

For the rest of the afternoon, until the sky began to grow dark, George and his friends kept on sledding. **He had snow in his underpants, up his nose, and even between his toes.** But that was okay with George. Cold and wet was how a normal, burp-free ten-year-old was *supposed* to be.

George set his sled up for one last run. *"Look out below!"* he shouted. *"HERE I COME!"*

That night as the boys got ready for bed, Kevin jumped around George's room, **punching at the air** and screaming *"KEEYAH!"* over and over again. Kevin was in his karate uniform. He kicked his leg up high in the air. "Oh yeah! I'm ready for tomorrow!"

That makes one of us, George thought to himself. Here it was Tuesday night, and he still hadn't figured out a way to cheer Kevin on at tomorrow's karate tournament and go to the *Schminess* show with Alex. **He couldn't choose between his two best friends.** No matter which one he chose, someone was going to be hurt.

"KEEYAH!" Kevin shouted again **for the one hundred and first time**.

"Wait until you see me break a board in two with my foot."

George wished Kevin could break him in two. Then George could be in both places at the same time.

Suddenly, George opened his eyes wide. He had an idea. "I'll be back in a minute." He ran downstairs for the newspaper. There were announcement ads with the addresses for both the *Schminess* show and the tournament.

"Are these places near each other?" George asked his dad.

"Right down the block from each other."

That was the answer George wanted to hear. Maybe there was a way he could be in two places at the same time. Or *almost* the same time. And if he did it just right, **neither Kevin nor Alex would ever have to know**.

Chapter 7

"KEEYAH!"

Kevin's shout filled the martial arts center. He gave a kick and—*crack!*—broke the board in two.

George leaped up in his seat and started cheering loudly so Kevin could hear him. Kevin bowed to the karate master, took the two pieces of wood in his hands, and went to sit on the sideline with the other contestants.

Now Kevin's back was to the audience. **That was George's cue!** He jumped out of his seat, threw on his coat, and headed for the door.

The hall where the *Schminess* exhibit

was being held was right down the block. Quickly, George ran outside and headed for the other end of the street.

George didn't stop. He couldn't. Alex was waiting.

"Dude, you're late," Alex said when George met up with him a few minutes later.

"Sorry." George huffed and puffed as he caught his breath. "I lost track of time." There. **That wasn't exactly a lie.**

"At least you're here now," Alex said. "Where's Kevin?"

"He . . . uh . . . couldn't come." *That isn't exactly a lie, either*, George thought.

Alex didn't seem disappointed about not seeing Kevin. "My ABC gum ball's in a garbage bag," Alex told George. "It's **way too big** to carry in my backpack now."

"Impressive!" George exclaimed.

"So you want to check out the competition? The record-holding gum ball is down that aisle," Alex said, pointing. "Or we could start at the guy with the beard that reaches the floor. Or maybe . . ."

There was **no way** George could visit a lot of exhibits and get back in time to watch Kevin spar against another green belt. But of course he didn't tell Alex that. Instead he said, "Why don't we go talk to the *Schminess* guys before there's a big line?"

"I don't know . . . I'm kind of nervous," Alex admitted.

"We're going together," George told him. **"I've got your back.** You'll be cool."

I'M THE GUY WITH THE **BEARD** THAT REACHES THE **FLOOR** and then Some!

"If you say so." Alex didn't sound very sure.

"I say so," George insisted. He looked at his watch. "Come on. Let's hurry."

Fifteen minutes later, Alex was still talking about his gum ball to the *Schminess* guys. And talking. **And talking.** Alex didn't act like a kid who was nervous at all.

But *George* was nervous that he would miss Kevin's next event if he didn't leave soon. **He really had to go.**

Go! That was it!

"Um, excuse me, Alex," George interrupted. "I have to go."

"Go?" Alex asked him. "Where?"

The guy from *Schminess* said, "I think your friend's telling you he has to go to the men's room."

"Oh," Alex said. "You need me to go with you?"

Alex thought George was about to burp! But that wasn't it at all.

"Nah, you keep talking," George told him. "I'll meet you at the world's smallest man."

"Okay," Alex said. "Give me a few minutes."

George smiled as he raced off. He hadn't lied to his best friend. He'd just said he had to go. Which he did. Alex didn't suspect a thing. **The plan was working perfectly.**

George was out of breath and sweating when he got back to the martial arts center. But it was so cold outside that the sweat on his face was starting to freeze. **Instead of icicles, he had _sweat_sicles**. _Yuck!_

Kevin was already in the middle of the floor, fighting against another boy. He turned and gave his opponent **a roundhouse kick**.

"Point," the judge said, gesturing toward Kevin.

Kevin's opponent let out a strong forward kick, which landed in the middle of Kevin's chest protector.

"Point." The judge was now gesturing toward the other boy.

Then Kevin let loose a series of **sharp kicks and punches**.

"Point," the judge said, gesturing toward Kevin. "And winner!"

George let out a cheer. He made it extra loud so he

could be sure Kevin knew he was there. Then George headed for the door.

The wind was blowing really hard as George raced to the *Schminess* show. His eyes were tearing from the cold. **Sweatsicles were forming on his face.** But George kept running as fast as his feet could carry him. Nothing was going to get in the way of his getting to the *Schminess* exhibit.

Nothing except Alex, that is.

"Wait up!" Alex shouted as he spotted George running down the street. "I've been looking all over for you."

Uh-oh.

"Why did you leave?" Alex asked. He sounded mad.

"Me?" George asked. "I . . . uh . . . well . . . I was out here looking for you."

Okay, *that* one was a lie. But what could he say?

"Why would you look out here?" Alex demanded. "We said we would meet by the world's smallest man, which is where I was standing for **a really, really long time**."

"Well, you see, the thing is . . ." George started, not sure what to say.

"There you are!"

Both George and Alex turned around

SCHMINESS EVENT

just in time to see Kevin coming down the street.

Uh-oh . . . again.

"What are you doing out here?" Kevin asked. "You missed seeing me win my division in the sparring contest."

"No. I saw you fighting . . . ," George began.

"What? George has been with me at the *Schminess Book of World Records* exhibit!" Alex told Kevin.

Kevin said, "No, he wasn't. George was at the karate tournament with me."

Both boys looked at George. **"Weren't you?"** they asked at the exact same time.

George was trapped. "I was at the tournament," he told Kevin. "And at the *Schminess* show," he told Alex.

"That's **scientifically impossible**," Alex said. "You can't be in two places at the same time."

"Right," George said. "But I was with you when you met with the *Schminess* people." He turned to Kevin. "And I saw you break your board and spar."

"But you're here now," Kevin said. "And they're giving out the trophies in, like, fifteen minutes. **Some best friend you are.**"

"I can go back and see you get your trophies . . . ," George began.

"I thought you were going back to the *Schminess* exhibits!" Alex said. "You should be with me. Especially after all *I've* been doing to help you cure **your you-know-what**!"

"What you-know-what?" Kevin demanded. "How come he knows about your you-know-what and I don't even know what the you-know-what is?"

"Because the you-know-what started in Beaver Brook, and you don't live here," Alex said. "George and I have a lot of secrets you don't know about."

"Not as many secrets as George and *I* have," Kevin said.

George was beginning to feel like the rope in the middle of his best friends' tug-of-war. "Stop it, guys! I'm friends with both of you!"

"So are you going to tell me what the **you-know-what** is or not?" Kevin demanded.

George gulped. What was he supposed to do now? If he didn't tell Kevin, Kevin would probably never talk to him again. But if he did tell him, he might think George was crazy. A magical super burp sounded kind of nuts, unless you were the kid who was burping it.

"Well, the thing is, Kev," he began, "ever since I came to Beaver Brook, I've been having **this problem** . . ."

Chapter 8

"Happy New Year!" George shouted
as he and Kevin greeted Alex at the door
on New Year's Eve. He blew into his
noisemaker. *Toot!*

"Hi, guys," Alex said.

"Here's a noisemaker for you," Kevin
said. "It's NBB."

"NBB?" Alex asked him.

"Never been blown," Kevin said.

Alex laughed. "Good one, dude."

George grinned. He was really glad his
two best buds were finally getting along.
After he'd explained what was going on,
Alex and George had gone to the karate
tournament to see Kevin get his trophies.

And then all three of them had gone back to the *Schminess* exhibit. After spending the whole afternoon together, Alex and Kevin had even teamed up to try to **find a cure for the super burp**.

George tooted his horn and then led Alex and Kevin into the living room. The guys made their way past the cheese balls, around the cut-up vegetables, behind the cookies, and over to the corner of the room where they could talk without any of the adults hearing.

"I've had George blowing into his noisemaker since this morning," Kevin told Alex. "I figure if the air is going out of his body, it can't all bubble up inside of him."

George blew into the noisemaker. *Toot.*

"George, that's enough," his mom called to him from the other side of the room. "You're making everyone crazy with that thing."

"They'd go crazier if the super burp came out," George told his friends.

"That's for sure," Alex agreed. "Kevin's idea about blowing air out is good."

Kevin smiled proudly.

"And I have another idea," Alex continued. He pulled a paper with a graph on it out of his pocket. "I've been keeping track of your burps the past few weeks. This green bar is the burp that almost came out on Jumping Mouse Lane. Remember?"

George nodded. **"I remember *every* burp.** Even the ones that don't make it out."

"Well, you did somersaults that day," Alex said. "And that stopped the burp. I'm

not sure why. Maybe it's because **all the rolling** flattened the bubbles."

"Kind of how we used a rolling pin to flatten the dough for the cookies we made this morning," Kevin suggested. He turned to George. "Blow."

George blew into his noisemaker. *Toot!*

"George! I told you to cut that out," his mother shouted across the room.

Alex folded the chart and put it in his pocket. "Try the somersault thing," he said.

George got down on the floor and did a forward roll—**right into the leg of his mom's friend Mrs. Gottelheimer.**

"Ouch!" Mrs. Gottelheimer said. "George, what are you doing?"

"Um . . . a somersault?" George said.

"Why?"

George didn't answer. Instead, he blew into his noisemaker. *Toot.*

Mrs. Gottelheimer **shook her head** and walked away.

"Feel any burps coming on?" Alex asked George.

George shook his head. "I'm bubble-free."

"Great!" Alex said. "By my **scientific calculations**, if you keep somersaulting—"

"And blowing," Kevin interrupted.

"Right, and blowing," Alex agreed, "you will make it through New Year's Eve without a **you-know-what**."

That sounded great to George. He blew into his **noisemaker**. *Toot.* Then he did a **double somersault**. *Flip. Flip.*

"I'm hungry," Kevin said. "Where are those pigs in a blanket?"

"They're in the kitchen," George said. He somersaulted his way to the kitchen, stopping every now and then to give his noisemaker a toot.

Toot. Toot. Flip. Flip. Toot. Toot. Flip. Flip.

"Ouch!" That came from George's dad. George had just **rolled right onto his foot**.

"Sorry," George apologized.

Two burp-free hours later, George's mother called out from the living room, "Only ten minutes until the ball drops in

Times Square. I'm turning on the TV."

"I want to see this!" Kevin shouted. "I've never been allowed to stay up until midnight before."

"Me neither," Alex said.

George's two best friends walked toward the living room. George followed them, but it was hard to keep up. He couldn't roll as fast as they could walk.

Toot! Flip. Toot! Flip. To—

Suddenly George stopped tooting. He stopped rolling. **He had to.** There were too many bubbles in his belly for him to even move. Already they had ping-ponged their way up to his chest and bing-bonged their way into his mouth and . . .

It was the last burp of the year. **And it**

was a whopper!

George's feet sprang into action, running through the house and heading for the hall closet.

"Whoa! George, slow down," his dad said as George passed him in the hall. "We still have a few minutes until New Year's."

But burps can't tell time. They only know now! And right now, the super burp was making George's hands grab a basketball from the closet. **Then he popped out of the closet and started dribbling down the hall.**

Bounce! Bounce! Bounce!

"George! There's no ball-playing in the house!" his mother warned.

182

But George's ears weren't listening.

Bounce! Bounce! Bounce! George's hands kept dribbling. His feet ran upstairs.

"It's time for the ball drop!" George's mouth shouted from the top of the stairs.

Everyone at the party looked up.

"What's George doing?" Mrs. Gottelheimer wondered out loud.

"Look out below!" George's mouth shouted as his hands tossed the ball down toward the crowd below.

Immediately, George's pals **leaped into action**. Kevin caught the ball in midair. Alex raced up the stairs and pushed George into his room before he could cause any more trouble. Then Kevin burst into the room and shut the door behind them.

Whoosh! Suddenly, George felt something pop in the bottom of his belly. All the air rushed out of him. The super burp was gone.

"You're just lucky Alex and I were here to stop you from doing anything worse," Kevin told him.

That was true. **George *was* lucky to have two amazing best friends.** With Alex and Kevin helping him, maybe this would be the Year of the Cure.

George smiled and opened his mouth to say "Happy new year!" **And that was exactly what came out.**

"Dude, that was a big burp," Alex said.

"You are definitely **the burping king**," Kevin agreed.

"Great," George grumbled.

"Come on," Kevin said. "You just burped in the new year. How many kids can say that?"

Only one. **George Brown, the amazing burping boy!** Too bad *Schminess* didn't have a category for that!

About the Author

Nancy Krulik is the author of more than 150 books for children and young adults including three *New York Times* best sellers and the popular Katie Kazoo, Switcheroo books. She lives in New York City with her family, and many of George Brown's escapades are based on things her own kids have done. (No one delivers a good burp quite like Nancy's son, Ian!) Nancy's favorite thing to do is laugh, which comes in pretty handy when you're trying to write funny books!

About the Illustrator

Aaron Blecha was raised by a school of giant squid in Wisconsin and now lives with his family by the English seaside. He works as an artist designing toys, animating cartoons, and illustrating books, including the Zombiekins and The Rotten Adventures of Zachary Ruthless series. You can enjoy more of his weird creations www.monstersquid.com.